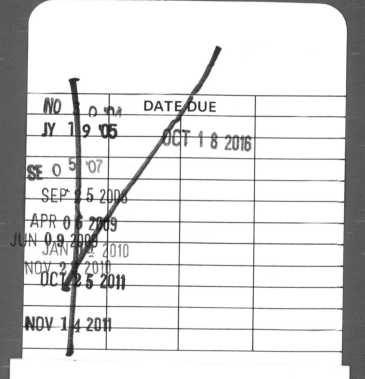

Copyright © 2002 by Nord-Süd Verlag AG, Gossau Zürich, Switzerland
First published in Switzerland under the title *Im Wald ist Platz für alle!*
English translation © 2003 by North-South Books Inc., New York

All rights reserved. No part of this book may be reproduced or utilized in
any form or by any means, electronic or mechanical, including photocopying,
recording, or any information storage and retrieval system,
without permission in writing from the publisher.

First published in the United States, Great Britain, Canada,
Australia, and New Zealand in 2003 by North-South Books,
an imprint of Nord-Süd Verlag AG, Gossau Zürich, Switzerland.

Distributed in the United States by North-South Books Inc., New York.

Library of Congress Cataloging-in-Publication Data is available.
A CIP catalogue record for this book is available from The British Library.
ISBN 0-7358-1681-6 (trade edition) 10 9 8 7 6 5 4 3 2 1
ISBN 0-7358-1682-4 (library edition) 10 9 8 7 6 5 4 3 2 1

For more information about our books, and the authors and artists
who create them, visit our web site: www.northsouth.com

Printed in Germany

There's Room in the Forest for Everyone

By Udo Weigelt
Illustrated by Gianluca Garofalo

Translated by Martina Rasdeuschek-Simmons

E

North-South Books
New York / London

One morning, Freddy the squirrel looked out of his hole. To his surprise, there sat another squirrel!

"Hello!" called the stranger. "My name is Morris. What's yours?"

"Freddy," said Freddy. "What do you want here, Morris?"

"I've lost my home," said Morris. "I'm looking for a new one."

"You aren't going to stay *here*?" asked Freddy, outraged.

"Why, yes," said Morris. "Your forest is so big. There are plenty of nuts, and the animals here seem very nice."

"Well, *I'm* not nice," snapped Freddy. "And *I'm* the squirrel here. This is my forest, and those are my nuts!"

"But surely there's enough for everyone," said Morris.

"No, there's not!" shouted Freddy, and he hurled a nut at Morris, who quickly leaped out of the way.

"Two squirrels in the forest—what a ridiculous idea!" muttered Freddy.

The next day, Freddy had new reasons to be angry.
Morris had moved into the tree right next to Freddy's.
A few days before a man had come and painted a big
red X on the tree, and Morris liked the X so much he
decided to settle there.

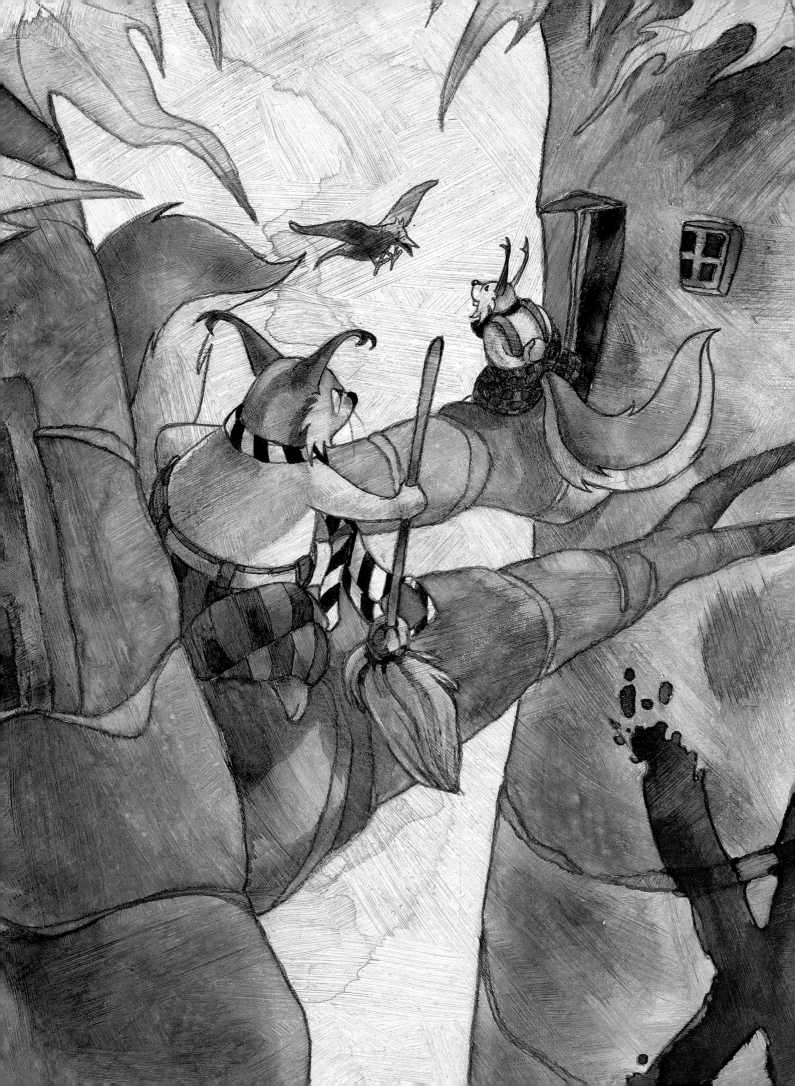

Freddy was bursting with rage. He gathered the other animals together and demanded that Morris be forced to move away. "One squirrel in the forest is enough," he said. "And I was here first."

But the other animals didn't see it that way.
"This is a big forest," said the wild boar. "Why,
there's enough room here for three squirrels."
The other animals nodded in agreement.
"All right!" shouted Freddy. "Then *I'll* move away.
I thought you were my friends, but I guess you like
Morris better."

Freddy ran into his hole and locked the door.
The animals knocked on his door and called his
name, but Freddy pretended not to hear them.

Sadly, Freddy packed his bag. His feelings were
hurt, but he would never admit it to the other animals.

Suddenly Freddy heard loud voices outside. He peeked out and saw a group of men gathered below him.

"That's the tree," said one of them. "Over there, with the red X."

"You're right, this tree is sick," said another. "It's a shame. But if we don't cut it down, other trees could get infected."

The men set to work.

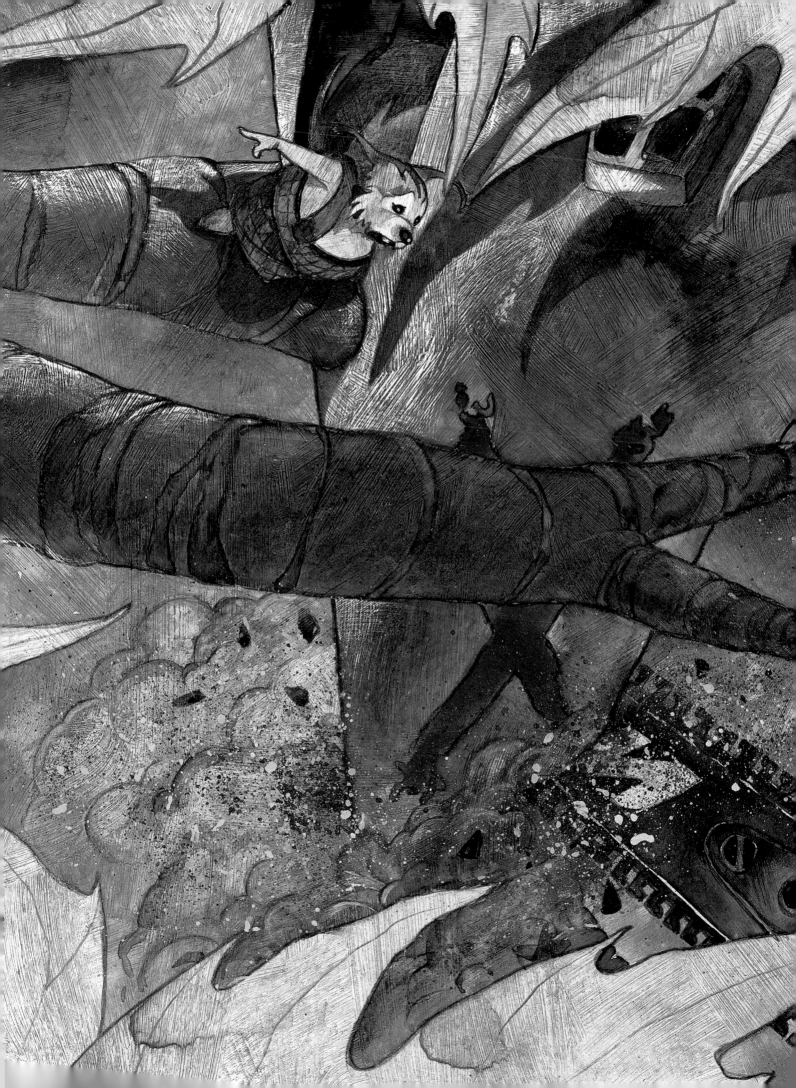

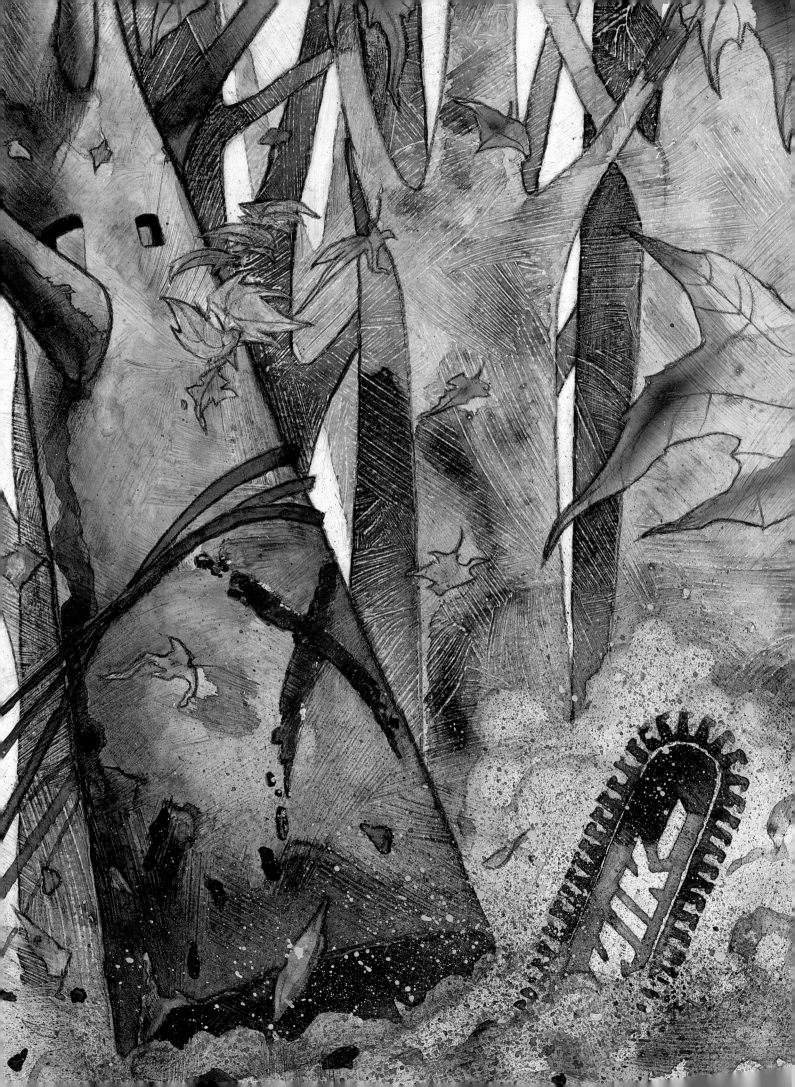

One of the workmen started a loud chain saw and began cutting, while the others made sure that the tree fell in the right direction.

"What are you doing?" cried Morris. "My new home! My nuts!"

But his frantic words were lost in the roar of the chain saw. Finally, there was a loud crack—and with a crash, the tree fell to the ground.

"Ha!" Freddy cried. "That serves Morris right."

But it was strange. Instead of being happy, Freddy found himself thinking about the poor squirrel who once again had lost his home.

Morris sat beside the fallen tree. Freddy cast a furtive glance at him and saw that he was crying.

Hmm, Freddy thought, that's not really what I wanted. . . . He hesitated. But not for long.

And so it happened that Morris found himself sitting in Freddy's home.

"So," Freddy said firmly, "from now on you'll live here with me. I have plenty of nuts—enough to last us both through the winter."

"But," Morris sniffled, "I thought you didn't like me and that you were going to move away."

"Well . . . I changed my mind," muttered Freddy, shuffling his feet in embarrassment.

"Oh," said Morris, "you mean we're friends now?"

Freddy thought it over. "Oh, all right, yes, we're friends!" he said gruffly. And even though he said it with a scowl, Freddy's eyes were shining happily.